THE BIG SNEEZE

by WILLIAM VAN HORN

SCHOLASTIC INC.
New York Toronto London Auckland Sydney Tokyo

To Eva Moore—
Where would Charlie and Fred
be without her?

No part of this publication may be reproduced in whole or in part, or stored
in a retrieval system, or transmitted in any form or by any means, electronic, mechanical,
photocopying, recording, or otherwise, without written permission of the publisher.
For information regarding permission, write to Scholastic Inc.,
730 Broadway, New York, NY 10003.

ISBN 0-590-33425-5

Reading level is determined by using the Spache Readability Formula.
2.0 signifies low 2nd-grade level.

Copyright © 1985 by William Van Horn.
All rights reserved. Published by Scholastic Inc.

12 11 10 9 8 7 6 5 4 3 2 1   1   5 6 7 8 9 / 8 0/9

Printed in the U.S.A.
11

Contents

The Big Sneeze

Bert Brontosaur was taking a walk.
It was spring and
the flowers were out.
"Those flowers smell
good enough to eat!" he said.
So he ate them.

He sniffed at some other flowers.
"These flowers just smell
good enough to smell."
He took a deep breath and sniffed.
The flowers made his nose itch.

"Aa . . . aa . . . choo!"
he sneezed once.
"Aa . . . aa . . . aa . . . choo!"
he sneezed twice.
Then —
"AA . . . AA . . ."

Bert sneezed himself right into
the pockleberry bushes.

Two small dinosaurs were
picking berries on the other side.
They were Bert's cousins,
Charlie and Fred.

"Hey, what's going on, Bert?"
cried Fred.

"I've got the sneezes," said Bert.
"And I can't stop."

"Aa . . . Aaa . . . Aaaaaaa . . .

CHOO!"

"Goodness, Bert," said Charlie.
"With sneezes like that, you could
sneeze up a storm!"

It so happened that the sky was
growing dark and stormy-looking.
But the three dinosaurs didn't
notice anything.
They were waiting to see if Bert
would sneeze again.

"Oh, oh," said Bert.
"I think this is going to be the
biggest, baddest,
most awful sneeze ever!"

Bert snorted and sniffed.
He sputtered and whoofed.
He drew in his breath . . .
"Aaaa . . . Aaaaaaa . . ."

Fred and Charlie ran for cover.
Just then the stormy clouds
rolled in and a great gust
of wind came up behind Bert.

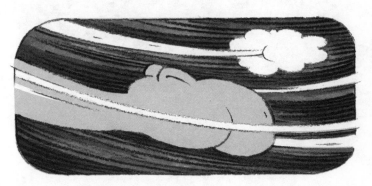

". . .CHOOOOOO!" went Bert.
"WHOOOOOOSH,"
went the wind.

The dinosaurs rolled
head over heels,

and heels over head.
They rolled all the way
to the Mud Flats
before they stopped.

The wind blew.
Rain poured.
Bert laughed.

"What's so funny, Bert?"
said Charlie.

"It looks like I really did
   sneeze up a storm," laughed Bert.
"Just like you said."

"Great," said Fred.
"Now let's see if you
   can sneeze us back home again."

But Bert was all sneezed out.
They had to walk.

By the time they got back home,
the storm was over and
the sun was out. The flowers
looked good enough to eat.

So Bert ate them.
But he was very careful
not to sniff them first.

It's a Bet

It was a warm summer day.
Birds were singing.
Bees were buzzing.
And Charlie Dinosaur was having
a fight with his brother Fred.
"I can TOO do lots of things
better than you!" said Charlie.

"Ha!" said Fred. "I bet you can't
run as fast as I can!"

"I bet I can!" said Charlie.

"All right," said Fred.
"I'll race you to the pond.
Then we'll see
who runs the fastest."

They got on their marks.
They got set.
And off they went.

Charlie ran like a rabbit —
and he won the race.

"See, I am the fastest," he said.

"Oh yeah!" said Fred.
"Well, I bet you
can't swim as fast as I can!"

"I bet I can!" said Charlie.

"All right," said Fred. "I'll race
you to the other side of the pond."

Charlie swam like a fish —

and he got to the other side first.
"I told you I
could do lots of things
better than you, Fred."

Fred wasn't going to give up.
"I bet you can't eat
as much as I can!
Because when it comes to eating,
this mouth is the world's champ!"

"Prove it," said Charlie.

"All right," said Fred.
"Let's see who can eat
the most pockleberries."
He grabbed a handful
and popped them into his mouth.
"Mmmm!" he said.
"Juicy and sweet.
I could eat a million of them!"

Fred gobbled pockleberries as fast
as he could pick them.

Charlie tried his best to keep up.

But soon Charlie was so full
of pockleberries,
he thought he would pop.
Fred went right on eating.
He didn't stop until he had eaten
all the pockleberries in sight.

"I think I ate too many berries,"
said Charlie. "I have a terrible
tummy-ache."

Fred snorted.
"I ate more than you did, Charlie.
and I bet I've got
a bigger tummy-ache too."

Charlie smiled.
"You know, Fred, for once
I bet you're right."

Snow Fun at All

There was cold in the air,
and Charlie shivered.
He and Fred were out for a walk,
and small flakes were beginning
to fall from the sky.
"It's starting to rain," said Charlie.
"I'm going home."

Fred laughed.
"Wait a minute, Charlie. This
isn't rain — it's *snow!*"

"I don't care what it is,"
said Charlie,
"I'm going home and get warm."

"But snow is *fun!*" said Fred.
"Watch, I'll show you."

Fred picked up a handful of snow
and dumped it on top of Charlie.
"Brrr!" said Charlie.
"It's cold and wet.
What's fun about that?"

"Don't be a party pooper," said Fred.
"Come on — I'll show you
how to slide down Slippery Hill.
Snow is great for sliding."

The snow fell harder as Charlie
and Fred climbed Slippery Hill.
"All you do," said Fred, "is run and
flop down on your belly. Watch!"

Fred ran, flopped down on his belly
and slid all the way to the bottom
of the hill.

"Your turn," he called to Charlie.
"Okay, okay!" grumbled Charlie.
"I'm coming." Charlie ran
and flopped down on his belly
just like Fred told him to.
But instead of sliding —

he rolled!

Soon Charlie was in the middle
of a snowball. It rolled
and bounced down the hill,
getting bigger and bigger until —

CRASH!

Fred laughed.

"I don't see anything funny
about this," said Charlie.
"I'm still cold,
I'm still wet,
and I'm still going home!"

That turned out to be
easier said than done.
The snow had gotten deeper.
Charlie and Fred had to plow
their way through it.
They could hardly see.

"This is really fun, Fred,"
said Charlie.

It was night
before they finally got home.
They had to dig
their way to the door.

But once they were inside
and sitting next to a fire,
Charlie was happy again.

"You know, Fred," he said,
"there is one thing
I *do* like about snow."

"Really?" said Fred. "What?"

"I like being out of it!" said Charlie,
and he moved closer to the fire.